To Sammy, Ripper, Sara, and Prim: a few of the best —L.A.T.

To Steve Malk —P.S.

Farrar Straus Giroux Books for Young Readers
175 Fifth Avenue, New York 10010

Text copyright © 2015 by Laurie Ann Thompson
Pictures copyright © 2015 by Paul Schmid
All rights reserved
Color separations by Bright Arts
Printed in China by South China Printing Co. Ltd.,
Dongguan City, Guangdong Province
First edition, 2015
10 9 8 7 6 5 4 3 2 1

mackids.com

Library of Congress Cataloging-in-Publication Data
Thompson, Laurie Ann.
    My dog is the best / Laurie Ann Thompson ; pictures by Paul Schmid.
  —First edition.
        pages cm
    Summary: A little boy identifies what makes his dog so special.
    ISBN 978-0-374-30051-7 (hardcover)
    [1. Dogs—Fiction.] I. Schmid, Paul, illustrator. II. Title.
PZ7.T371633My 2015264
[E]—dc23
                                            2013041347

Farrar Straus Giroux Books for Young Readers may be purchased for business or promotional use. For information on bulk purchases
please contact Macmillan Corporate and Premium Sales Department at (800) 221-7945 x5442 or by email at specialmarkets@macmillan.com.

My Dog Is the Best

yawn!

LAURIE ANN THOMPSON ★ Pictures by PAUL SCHMID

FARRAR STRAUS GIROUX / NEW YORK

My dog is the best. He does tricks.

He plays dead.

He rolls over.

My dog is the best. He is fun.

He plays ball.

He plays tug.

He plays chase.

My dog is the best. He is strong and brave.

He helps the firemen.

He scares away monsters.

My dog is the best. He is smart.

He listens to my stories.

He blows bubbles.

He reads books.

My dog is the best.
He makes me smile.

He gives hugs.

He is mine.

Woof!